FRIENDS ARE FUN

STEVE HENRY

I Like to Read®

HOLIDAY HOUSE • NEW YORK

Pete was alone.

And that was okay.

One day,
Turtle came.
"May I stay?"
said Turtle.

Pete said,
"Okay."

Dog came.

"May I stay?" said Dog.

Pete said,
"Okay."

They all played.

Elephant
came.

"May I stay?"
said Elephant.

What did Pete say?

Pete said, "Okay."

The friends played.

A storm came.

Elephant helped
her friends.

The storm ended.

The friends
were safe.

Elephant and Dog went. "Come again," said Pete.

Turtle stayed.

Pete was not alone.
And that was okay.